SILENT NIGHT:
THE WONDER OF CHRISTMAS

·SILENT NIGHT·

THE WONDER OF CHRISTMAS

Kathryn M. Patton, Editor

SILENT NIGHT

Joseph Mohr

Silent night! Holy night!
All is calm, all is bright.
Round yon virgin mother and Child.
Holy Infant, so tender and mild.
Sleep in heavenly peace,
Sleep in heavenly peace.

Silent night! Holy night!
Shepherds quake at the sight!
Glories stream from heaven afar;
Heavenly hosts sing Alleluia!
Christ, the Saviour, is born!
Christ, the Saviour, is born!

Silent night! Holy night!
Son of God, love's pure light.
Radiant beams from Thy holy face.
With the dawn of redeeming grace.
Jesus, Lord, at Thy birth!
Jesus, Lord, at Thy birth!

Silent night, holy night,
Wondrous star, lend thy light;
With the angels let us sing
Alleluia to our King.
Christ the Saviour is here,
Jesus the Saviour is here!

IDEALS PUBLICATIONS
NASHVILLE, TENNESSEE

ISBN 0-8249-5877-2

Published by Ideals Publications
A division of Guideposts
535 Metroplex Drive, Suite 250
Nashville, Tennessee 37211
www.idealsbooks.com

Publisher, Patricia A. Pingry
Book Editor, Kathryn M. Patton
Art Director, Eve DeGrie
Permissions Editor, Patsy Jay

Library of Congress Cataloging-in-Publication Data

The wonder of Christmas / edited by Kathryn M. Patton.
    p. cm.
  Includes index.
  ISBN 0-8249-5877-2 (alk. paper)
  1. Christmas. I. Patton, Kathryn M.
  BV45.W66 2004
  264'.031—dc22

                                                    2004015125

Printed and bound in U. S. A.

10 9 8 7 6 5 4 3 2 1

ACKNOWLEDGMENTS

BETJEMAN, JOHN. "Advent" from *Uncollected Poems* by John Betjeman. Published in 1982 by John Murray Ltd., Hodder Headline Group. Used by permission. CAUSLEY, CHARLES "Mary's Song" from *Collected Poems for Children*. Published by Macmillan. Used by permission of David Higham Assoc. CHESTERTON, G. K. "The House of Christmas" from *Poems* by G. K. Chesterton, 1915. Used by permission of A. P. Watt Ltd., on behalf of The Royal Literary Fund. COLQUHOUN, FRANK. "O God the Son" from *Contemporary Parish Prayers*. Published in 1975 by Hodder & Stoughton and used here with their permission. FARJEON, ELEANOR. "In the Week When Christmas Comes" and "For Christmas Day" from *Silver Sand and Snow* by Eleanor Farjeon. Published by Michael Joseph Ltd. Used by permission of David Higham Assoc. GOUDGE, ELIZABETH. "Now 'Tis Christmas" from *The Dean's Watch*. Published by Hodder and Stoughton. Used by permission of David Higham Assoc. HEINE, HEINRICH. "The Wise Men Ask the Children the Way" from *The Cherry Tree*. Translation by Geoffrey Grigson is used by permission of David Higham Assoc. HUGGETT, JOYCE. "A Christmas Prayer" from *The Complete book of Christian Prayer*. Copyright © 1995 by SPCK. Used by permission of The Continuum International Publishing Group. LEE, LAURIE. "Country Carols" from *The Illustrated Cider With Rosie* by Laurie Lee. Copyright © 1984. Crown Publishers, NY. Used by permission of PFD on behalf of the Estate of Laurie Lee. LUTHER, MARTIN. "From Heaven High" from *Christmas Carols and Their Stories*. Compiled by Christopher Idle. A Lion Book. Copyright © 1988. Translated from the German by Roland H. Bainton. NICHOLSON, NORMAN. "Carol for the Last Christmas Eve" from *Collected Poems* by Norman Nicholson, published by Faber and Faber, 1994. Used by permission of David Higham Assoc. SHAW, ISABEL. "Christmas Chant" from *Jack and Jill*, copyright © 1949 by Curtis Publishing. Used by permission of Children's Better Health Institute, Benjamin Franklin Literary & Medical Society. VANAUKEN, SHELDON. "The Heart of Mary" from *A Severe Mercy* by Sheldon Vanauken. Copyright © 1977, 1980 by the author. Published by HarperSanFrancisco. WEATHERHEAD, LESLIE D. "This Night of Nights" from *The Christmas Companion*. Edited by John Hadfield. Published by E. P. Dutton & Co., 1939. Used by permission of the author's Estate. Our sincere thanks to the Estate of Denis A. McCarthy for use of "Christmas Legends."

*Every effort has been made to establish ownership and use of each selection in this book. The publisher will be pleased to rectify any inadvertant errors or omissions in subsequent editions upon notification.

Images used: page 2 copyright by Erich Lessing/Art Resource, NY; page 129 by Smithsonian American Art Museum/Art Resource, NY; pages 31 and 157 by Gene Plaisted/The Crosiers; pages 17, 87, 107, and 135 by Christie's Images, NY; all other images by Fine Art Photographic Library, London.

CONTENTS

INTRODUCTION

Christmas has always been a holiday—a "holy day"—filled with wonder from first to last. It tells a wondrous story, outdoing the most fantastic fairy tales with its truth. It speaks of age-old prophecies fulfilled in a baby boy; it invites us to ponder with Mary the mystery of God becoming man; it asks us to follow the shepherds to find the King born in a stable. But added to the wonder of the Christmas story are the wonderful festivities and celebrations that adorn this time of "good-will toward men." Like the wise men who sought to worship Jesus, we too have our special Christmas services, where hushed and candlelit churches prepare joyfully for the coming of God's Son. And like the angels' song that was heard by the amazed shepherds, our songs and carols fill the Christmas season with awe and gladness.

On Christmas Eve in 1918, at the King's College Chapel in Cambridge, England, one lone voice was heard echoing sweetly from the rear of the medieval chapel, "Once in royal David's city . . ." Other voices soon joined in, the choir forming a processional down the aisle to take their places at the front. This was the beginning of a Christmas service, *The Festival of Lessons and Carols*, that continues today and is celebrated in churches all over the world. The service has been broadcast every Christmas Eve from the King's College Chapel to millions of yuletide listeners. It is arranged around nine "lessons," passages from Scripture from Genesis to John that extol the birth of the Prince of Peace, and is accompanied by Christmas's most beloved carols.

Capturing the wonder of Christmas, the following chapters are likewise arranged around these nine "lessons" and carols, celebrating the joy and majesty of the season that can be found nowhere else like in voices lifted up in song, church bells pealing out glad tidings, and the wonder of the Word that brings peace to all men.

—K. P.

ONCE IN ROYAL DAVID'S CITY

Cecil Frances Alexander

Henry J. Gauntlet

1. Once in roy-al Da-vid's cit-y stood a low-ly cat-tle shed,
2. He came down to earth from heav-en who is God and Lord of all,
3. And, through all His won-drous child-hood He would hon-or and o-bey,
4. And our eyes at last shall see Him, through His own re-deem-ing love;
5. Not in that poor low-ly sta-ble, with the ox-en stand-ing by,

Where a moth-er laid her ba-by in a man-ger for His bed;
And His shel-ter was a stab-le, and His cra-dle was a stall.
Love and watch the low-ly maid-en in whose gen-tle arms He lay;
For that child so dear and gen-tle is our Lord in heav'n a-bove;
We shall see Him, but in heav-en, set at God's right hand on high.

Ma-ry, lov-ing moth-er mild, Je-sus Christ, her lit-tle child.
With the poor, the scorned, the low-ly lived on earth our Sav-iour ho-ly.
Chris-tian chil-dren all must be mild, o-bed-ient, good as He.
And He leads His chil-dren on to the place where He is gone.
When, like stars, His chil-dren crowned, all in white shall wait a-round.

CHAPTER ONE

ANCIENT PROMISE

GENESIS 3:8-15, 17-19

And they heard the voice of the LORD God walking in the garden in the cool of the day: and Adam and his wife hid themselves from the presence of the LORD God amongst the trees of the garden. And the LORD God called unto Adam, and said unto him, Where art thou? And he said, I heard thy voice in the garden, and I was afraid, because I was naked; and I hid myself. And he said, Who told thee that thou wast naked? Hast thou eaten of the tree, whereof I commanded thee that thou shouldest not eat? And the man said, The woman whom thou gavest to be with me, she gave me of the tree, and I did eat. And the LORD God said unto the woman, What is this that thou hast done? And the woman said, The serpent beguiled me, and I did eat. And the LORD God said unto the serpent, Because thou hast done this, thou art cursed above all cattle, and above every beast of the field; upon thy belly shalt thou go, and dust shalt thou eat all the days of thy life: And I will put enmity between thee and the woman, and between thy seed and her seed; it shall bruise thy head, and thou shalt bruise his heel. And unto Adam he said, Because thou hast hearkened unto the voice of thy wife, and hast eaten of the tree, of which I commanded thee, saying, Thou shalt not eat of it: cursed is the ground for thy sake; in sorrow shalt thou eat of it all the days of thy life; Thorns also and thistles shall it bring forth to

Wishing you a merry Christmas.

thee; and thou shalt eat the herb of the field; In the sweat of thy face shalt thou eat bread, till thou return unto the ground; for out of it wast thou taken: for dust thou art, and unto dust shalt thou return.

THIS IS THE TRUTH SENT FROM ABOVE

Traditional

Traditional

1. This is the truth sent from a - bove,
2. The first thing which I do re - late
3. And we were heirs to end - less woes
4. And at that sea - son of the year
5. Thus He in love to us be - haved,

The truth of God, the God of love,
It that God did man cre - ate;
Till the Lord God did in - ter - pose;
Our blest Re - deem - er did ap - pear;
To show us how we must be saved;

There - fore don't turn me from your door
The next thing which to you I'd tell—
And so a prom - ise soon did run
Here He did live, and here did preach,
And if you want to know the way,

But heark - en all, both rich and poor.
Wo - man was made with man to dwell.
That He'd re - deem us by His Son.
And man y thou - sands what He did teach.
Be pleased to hear what He did say.

A Christmas Carol

Aubrey De Vere

They leave the land of gems and gold,
The shining portals of the East;
For Him, the woman's Seed foretold,
They leave the revel and the feast.

To earth their scepters they have cast,
And crowns by kings ancestral worn;
They track the lonely Syrian waste;
They kneel before the Babe new born.

O happy eyes that saw Him first;
O happy lips that kissed His feet:
Earth slakes at last her ancient thirst;
With Eden's joy her pulses beat.

True kings are those who thus forsake
Their kingdoms for the Eternal King;
Serpent, her foot is on thy neck;
Herod, thou writhest, but canst not sting.

He, He is King, and He alone
Who lifts that infant hand to bless;
Who makes His mother's knee His throne,
Yet rules the starry wilderness.

THOU THAT MADEST MORN
A. C. Swinburne

Thou whose birth on earth
Angels sang to men,
While the stars made mirth,
Saviour, at thy birth
This day born again.

As this night was bright
With thy cradle-ray,
Very light of light,
Turn the wild world's night
To thy perfect day.

Bid our peace increase,
Thou that madest morn;
Bid oppressions cease,
Bid the night be peace,
Bid the day be born.

PATAPAN
Bernard De La Monnoye

Willie, take your little drum,
With your whistle, Robin, come!
When we hear the fife and drum,
Ture-lure-lu, pata-pata-pan,
When we hear the fife and drum
Christmas should be frolicsome.

Thus the men of olden days
Loved the King of Kings to praise:
When they hear the fife and drum,
Ture-lure-lu, pata-pata-pan,
When they hear the fife and drum
Sure our children won't be dumb!

God and man are now become
More at one than fife and drum.
When you hear the fife and drum,
Ture-lure-lu, pata-pata-pan,
When you hear the fife and drum,
Dance and make the village hum!

NOW THAT THE TIME HAS COME
Author Unknown

Now that the time has come wherein
Our Saviour Christ was born,
The larder's full of beef and pork,
The granary's full of corn;

As God hath plenty to thee sent,
Take comfort of thy labours,
And let it never thee repent
To feed thy needy neighbors.

THE LORD AT FIRST DID ADAM MAKE

Traditional

Traditional

1. The Lord at first did A - dam make, out of the dust and clay;
2. And thus with - in the gar - den he com - mand - ed was to stay!
3. "For in the day that thou dost touch, or un - to it come nigh,
4. Now mark the good - ness of the Lord, which He to man - kind bore;
5. And now the tide is nigh at hand, in which our Sav - iour came;
6. Now, for the ben - e - fits that we en - joy from Heav'n a - bove,
7. And now the tide is nigh at hand, in which our Sav - iour came;

And in his nos - trils breath - ed life, as ho - ly scrip - tures
And we to him for stat - ute good these words the Lord did
Or if that thou shouldst eat there - of, then thou shalt sure - ly
His mer - cy soon He did ex - tend, lost man for to re -
Let us re - joice and mer - ry be, in keep - ing of the
Let us re - nounce all wick - ed - ness, and live in per - fect
Let us re - joice and mer - ry be in keep - ing of the

say: And then in E - den's Par - a - dise He
say, "The fruit that in the gar - den grows to
die." But A - dam he did take no heed to
store; And then, for to re - deem our souls from
same. Let's feed the poor and clothe the bare, and
love. Then shall we do Christ's own com - mand, e -
same; Let's feed the poor and hun - gry sort, and

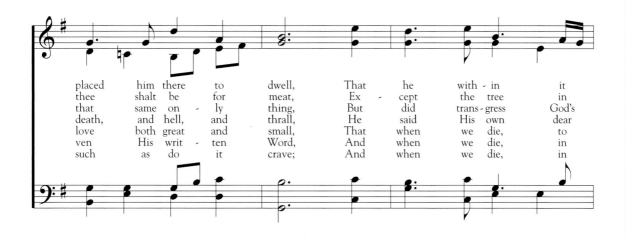

placed him there to dwell, That he with - in it
thee shalt be for meat, Ex - cept the tree in
that same on - ly thing, But did trans-gress God's dear
death, and hell, and thrall, He said His own dear
love both great and small, That when we die, to
ven His writ - ten Word, And when we die, in
such as do it crave; And when we die, in

should re - main, to dress and keep it well.
midst there - of, of which thou shalt not eat."
ho - ly laws, and soon was wrapp'd in sin.
Son should come, the Sav - iour of us all.
Heav'n at last our Lord may bring us all.
Heav'n we shall en - joy our liv - ing Lord.
Heav'n be sure our re - ward we shall have.

Now let good Chris - tians all be - gin a ho - ly life to live,

And to re - joice and mer - ry be, for this is Christ - mas Eve.

Wishing you
A Happy Christmas.

A Christmas Prayer
Robert Louis Stevenson

O God, our loving Father, help us to remember the birth of Jesus, that we may share in the song of the angels, the gladness of the shepherds, and the worship of the wise men. May the Christmas morning make us happy to be thy children, and the Christmas evening bring us to our beds with grateful thoughts, forgiving and forgiven, for Jesus' sake. Amen.

In the Week When Christmas Comes
Eleanor Farjeon

This is the week when Christmas comes.

Let every pudding burst with plums,
And every tree bear dolls and drums,
In the week when Christmas comes.

Let every hall have boughs of green,
With berries glowing in between,
In the week when Christmas comes.

Let every steeple ring a bell
With a joyful tale to tell,
In the week when Christmas comes.

Let every night put forth a star
To show us where the heavens are,
In the week when Christmas comes.

Let every stable have a lamb
Sleeping warm beside its dam,
In the week when Christmas comes.

This is the week when Christmas comes.

ADVENT
John Betjeman

The Advent wind begins to stir
With sea-like sounds in our Scotch fir,
It's dark at breakfast, dark at tea,
And in between we only see
Clouds hurrying across the sky
And rain-wet roads the wind blows dry
And branches bending to the gale
Against great skies all silver-pale.
The world seems travelling into space,
And travelling at a faster pace
Than in the leisured summer weather
When we and it sit out together,
For now we feel the world spin round
On some momentous journey bound—
Journey to what? to whom? to where?
The Advent bells call out 'Prepare,
Your world is journeying to the birth
Of God made Man for us on earth.'

INCARNATION
Charles H. Spurgeon

Christ is the great central fact in the world's history. To Him everything looks forward or backward. All the lines of history converge upon Him. All the great purposes of God culminate in Him. The greatest and most momentous fact which the history of the world records is the fact of His birth.

CHAPTER TWO

THE NATIONS BLESSED

GENESIS 22:15-18

And the angel of the Lord called unto Abraham out of heaven the second time, And said, By myself have I sworn, saith the Lord, for because thou hast done this thing, and hast not withheld thy son, thine only son: That in blessing I will bless thee, and in multiplying I will multiply thy seed as the stars of the heaven, and as the sand which is upon the sea shore; and thy seed shall possess the gate of his enemies; And in thy seed shall all the nations of the earth be blessed; because thou hast obeyed my voice.

ON CHRISTMAS NIGHT

Traditional

Arr. R. Vaughn Williams

The Wassail Bowl.

News of our mer - ci - ful King's birth.
All for to see the new - born King.
Now and for - ev - er - more A - men."

Now 'Tis Christmas

Elizabeth Goudge

Every year, at half-past five on Christmas Eve . . . the cathedral bells rang out. They pealed for half an hour, and all over the city, and in all the villages to which the wind carried the sound of the bells, they knew that Christmas had begun. People in the fen wrapped cloaks about them and went out of doors and stood looking toward the city. This year it was bitterly cold but the wind had swept the clouds away and the cathedral on its hill towered up among the stars, light shining from its windows. Below it the twinkling city lights were like clustering fireflies about its feet. The tremendous bells' music that was rocking the tower and pealing through the city was out here as lovely and far away as though it rang out from the stars themselves, and it caught at mens' hearts. "Now 'tis Christmas," they said to each other, as their forebears had said for centuries past, looking toward the city on the hill and the great church that was as much a part of their blood and bones as the fen itself. "'Tis Christmas," they said, and went back happy to their homes.

In the city, as soon as the bells started, everyone began to get ready. Then from nearly every house, family parties came out and made their way up the steep streets toward the cathedral. Quite small children were allowed to stay up for the carol service, and they chattered like sparrows as they stumped along buttoned into their thick coats, the boys gaitered and mufflered, the girls with muffs and fur bonnets. It was the custom in the city to put lighted candles in the windows on Christmas Eve and their light, and the light of the street lamps, made of the streets ladders of light leaning against the hill. The grown-ups found them Jacob's ladders tonight, easy to climb, for the bells and the children tugged them up.

Nearly everyone entered by the west door, for they loved the thrill of crossing the green under the moon and stars, and mounting the steps and gazing up at the west front, and then going in through the Porch of Angels beneath . . . the pealing bells. . . . There were lights in the nave but they could do no more than splash pools of gold here and there, they could not illumine the shadows above or the dim unlighted chantries and half-seen tombs. The great pillars soared into darkness and the aisles narrowed to twilight. Candles twinkled in the choir and the high altar with its flowers was ablaze with them, but all the myriad of flames were no more than seed pearls embroidered on a dark cloak. . . . All things went out into mystery. The crowd of tiny human creatures flowed up the nave and onto the benches. The sound of their feet, their whispering voices and rustling garments, was lost in the vastness. The music of the organ flowed over them and they were still.

GLORY TO GOD IN THE HIGHEST

THE FEAST DAY OF YOUR BIRTH
Ephraim the Syrian

The feast day of your birth resembles you, Lord,
Because it brings joy to all humanity.
Old people and infants alike enjoy your day.
Your day is celebrated from generation to generation.
Kings and emperors may pass away,
And the festivals to commemorate them soon lapse.
But your festival will be remembered till the end of time.
Your day is a means and a pledge of peace.
At your birth heaven and earth were reconciled,
Since you came from heaven to earth on that day.
You forgave our sins and wiped away our guilt.
You gave us so many gifts on your birthday:
A treasure chest of spiritual medicines for the sick;
Spiritual light for those that are blind;
The cup of salvation for the thirsty;
The bread of life for the hungry.
In the winter when the trees are bare,
You give us the most succulent spiritual fruit.
In the frost when the earth is barren,
You bring new hope to our souls.
In December when seeds are hidden in the soil,
The staff of life springs forth from the virgin womb.

DING DONG MERRILY ON HIGH

George Ratcliffe Woodward

Traditional

Glo - - - - - - - - - - - - - - - - ri - a, Ho -

san - na in ex - cel - sis.

A Christmas Chime
Kathleen Kavanagh

Keep time, keep time, glad Christmas chime!
Louder, louder sing thy song sublime;
Ne'er half enough can e'er be told
Of that dear story, sweet and old.
Hark, men and women—children too—
List to the wondrous tale anew,
How long ago, in land afar,
The shepherd saw the shining star,
Heard echoed strains of harp and lyre
Attuned to thrill of angel choir.

Keep time, keep time, wild, joyful chime
Bid every heart keep Christmas time—
Let there be none so worn and weary,
Let there be none so lone and dreary,
That thy rich music may not fill
With happiness and fond good will,
With just a bit of hope and cheer,
A firmer trust in heaven near,
A sense of sacred, new-found rest,
That Jesus sleeps on Mary's breast.

Keep time, keep time, blest Christmas chime!
Repeat thy message true, sublime,
Unto the mighty, to the lowly,
Unto the sinner, to the holy:
Bid them live on in gentle peace,
Their strife and hatred all to cease;
And bid them come, not, as of old,
With frankincense, myrrh, gems, and gold,
But with the nobler—love's own proffer—
Unto their God their hearts to offer.

CHRISTMAS BELLS
Henry Wadsworth Longfellow

I heard the bells on Christmas day
Their old familiar carols play,
And wild and sweet
The words repeat
Of 'Peace on earth, good will to men!'

And though how, as the day had come,
The belfries of all Christendom
Had rolled along
The unbroken song,
Of 'Peace on earth, good will to men!'

Till ringing, singing on its way,
The world revolved from night to day—
A voice, a chime,
A chant sublime,
Of 'Peace on earth, good will to men!'

And in despair I bowed my head:
'There is no peace on earth,' I said,
'For hate is strong
And mocks the song
Of peace on earth, good will to men!'

Then pealed the bells more loud and deep:
'God is not dead; nor doth he sleep!
The wrong shall fail,
The right prevail,
With peace on earth, good will to men!'

· CHAPTER THREE ·

KING OF KINGS

Isaiah 7:14b; 9:2,6,7

ehold, a virgin shall conceive, and bear a son, and shall call his name Immanuel. The people that walked in darkness have seen a great light: they that dwell in the land of the shadow of death, upon them hath the light shined. For unto us a child is born, unto us a son is given: and the government shall be upon his shoulder: and his name shall be called Wonderful, Counsellor, The mighty God, The everlasting Father, The Prince of Peace. Of the increase of his government and peace there shall be no end, upon the throne of David, and upon his kingdom, to order it, and to establish it with judgment and with justice from henceforth even for ever. The zeal of the LORD of hosts will perform this.

IT CAME UPON THE MIDNIGHT CLEAR

Edmund Hamilton Sears

Richard S. Willis

PRINCE OF PEACE
Philip Doddridge

Hark the glad sound! the Saviour comes,
The Saviour promised long:
Let every heart prepare a throne
And every voice a song.

He comes the prisoners to release
In Satan's bondage held;
The gates of brass before him burst,
The iron fetters yield.

He comes the broken heart to bind,
The bleeding soul to cure,
And with the treasures of his grace
To enrich the humble poor.

Our glad hosannas, Prince of peace,
Thy welcome shall proclaim,
And heaven's eternal arches ring
With thy beloved name.

CHRISTMAS
Washington Irving

Of all the old festivals . . . that of Christmas awakens the strongest and most heartfelt associations. There is a tone of solemn and sacred feeling that blends with our conviviality and lifts the spirit to a state of hallowed and elevated enjoyment. The services of the Church about this season are extremely tender and inspiring. They dwell on the beautiful story of the origin of our faith and the pastoral scenes that accompanied its announcement. They gradually increase in fervor and pathos during the season of Advent, until they break forth in full jubilee on the morning that brought peace and good will to men. I do not know a grander effect of music on the moral feelings than to hear the full choir and the pealing organ performing a Christmas anthem in a cathedral, and filling every part of the vast pile with triumphant harmony.

O Come, O Come, Emmanuel

Trans. John Mason Neale

Arr. University of Wales

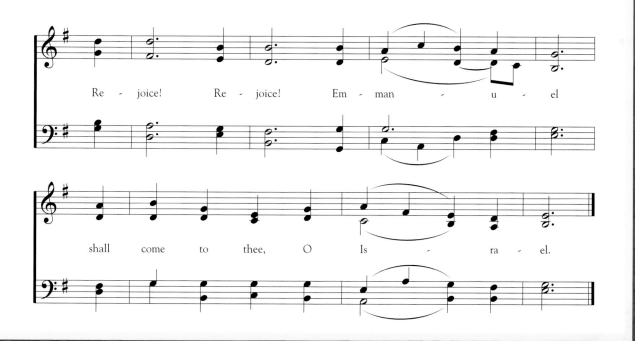

Re - joice! Re - joice! Em - man - u - el

shall come to thee, O Is - ra - el.

PRAYER UPON CHRISTMASTIME
Bernard of Clairvaux

Let your goodness, Lord, appear to us, that we, made in your image, conform ourselves to it. In our own strength we cannot imitate your majesty, power, and wonder; nor is it fitting for us to try. But your mercy reaches from the heavens, through the clouds, to the earth below. You have come to us as a small child, but you have brought us the greatest of all gifts, the gift of eternal love. Caress us with your tiny hands, embrace us with your tiny arms, and pierce our hearts with your soft, sweet cries.

CHRISTMAS TONIGHT
Phillips Brooks

Everywhere, everywhere, Christmas tonight!
Christmas in lands of the fir tree and pine,
Christmas in lands of the palm tree and vine,
Christmas where snow peaks stand solemn and white,
Christmas where cornfields stand sunny and bright.
Christmas where children are hopeful and gay,
Christmas where old men are patient and gray,
Christmas where peace, like a dove in his flight,
Broods o'er brave men in the thick of the fight;
Everywhere, everywhere, Christmas tonight!
For the Christ-child who comes is the Master of all;
No palace too great, no cottage too small.

COME, THOU LONG EXPECTED JESUS

Charles Wesley

Come, Thou long expected Jesus,
Born to set Thy people free;
From our fears and sins release us,
Let us find our rest in Thee.
Israel's strength and consolation,
Hope of all the earth Thou art;
Dear desire of every nation,
Joy of every longing heart.

Born Thy people to deliver,
Born a child and yet a King,
Born to reign in us forever,
Now Thy gracious kingdom bring.
By Thine own eternal Spirit
Rule in all our hearts alone;
By Thine all sufficient merit,
Raise us to Thy glorious throne.

THE TIME DRAWS NEAR

Alfred Lord Tennyson

The time draws near the birth of Christ:
The moon is hid; the night is still;
The Christmas bells from hill to hill
Answer each other in the mist.

Four voices of four hamlets round,
From far and near, on mead and moor,
Swell out and fail, as if a door
Were shut between me and the sound:

Each voice four changes on the wind,
That now dilate, and now decrease,
Peace and goodwill, goodwill and peace,
Peace and goodwill, to all mankind.

Rise, happy morn; rise, holy morn;
Draw forth the cheerful day from night:
O Father, touch the East, and light
The light that shone when Hope was born.

CHAPTER FOUR

PEACE ON EARTH

Isaiah 11:1-4, 6-9

nd there shall come forth a rod out of the stem of Jesse, and a Branch shall grow out of his roots: And the spirit of the LORD shall rest upon him, the spirit of wisdom and understanding, the spirit of counsel and might, the spirit of knowledge and of the fear of the LORD; And shall make him of quick understanding in the fear of the LORD: and he shall not judge after the sight of his eyes, neither reprove after the hearing of his ears: But with righteousness shall he judge the poor, and reprove with equity for the meek of the earth: and he shall smite the earth: with the rod of his mouth, and with the breath of his lips shall he slay the wicked. The wolf also shall dwell with the lamb, and the leopard shall lie down with the kid; and the calf and the young lion and the fatling together; and a little child shall lead them. And the cow and the bear shall feed; their young ones shall lie down together: and the lion shall eat straw like the ox. And the sucking child shall play on the hole of the asp, and the weaned child shall put his hand on the cockatrice' den. They shall not hurt nor destroy in all my holy mountain: for the earth shall be full of the knowledge of the LORD, as the waters cover the sea.

A Holy Happy Christmas to you.

Lo, How a Rose Ere Blooming

Trans. Theodore Baker

Arr. Michael Praetorius

THE OXEN
Thomas Hardy

Christmas Eve, and twelve of the clock.
'Now they are all on their knees,'
An elder said, as we sat in a flock
By the embers in fireside ease.

We pictured the meek, mild creatures, where
They dwelt in their strawy pen.
Nor did it occur to one of us there
To doubt they were kneeling then.

So fair a fancy few would weave
In these years! Yet, I feel
If someone said, on Christmas Eve,
'Come; see the oxen kneel

'In the lonely barton by yonder coomb,
Our childhood used to know,'
I should go with him in the gloom,
Hoping it might be so.

HEAP ON MORE WOOD!
Sir Walter Scott

Heap on more wood!—the wind is chill;
But let it whistle as it will,
We'll keep our Christmas merry still.

A Christmas Carol
Charles Kingsley

It chanced upon the merry, merry Christmas Eve
I went sighing past the church, across the moorland dreary—
"Oh! Never sin and want and woe this earth will leave,
And the bells but mock the wailing round they sing so cheery.
How long, O Lord! how long before Thou come again?
Still in cellar, and in garret, and on moorland dreary,
The orphans moan, and widows weep, and poor men toil in vain,
Till earth is sick of hope deferred, though Christmas bells be cheery."

Then arose a joyous clamor from the wildfowl on the mere,
Beneath the stars, across the snow, like clear bells ringing,
And a voice within cried, "Listen! Christmas carols even here!
Though thou be dumb, yet o'er their work the stars and snows are singing.
Blind! I live, I love, I reign; and all the nations through
With the thunder of My judgments even now are ringing.
Do thou fulfill thy work but as yon wildfowl do,
Thou wilt hear no less the wailing, yet hear through it angels singing."

Christmas Voices
William Shakespeare

Some say, that ever 'gainst that season comes
Wherein our Saviour's birth is celebrated,
This bird of dawning singeth all night long;
And then, they say, no spirit dare stir abroad;
The nights are wholesome; then no planets strike,
No fairy takes, nor witch hath power to charm,
So hallowed and so gracious is the time.

THE HOLLY AND THE IVY

Traditional

Arr. John Stainer

Christmas Legends
Denis A. McCarthy

Christmas morn, the legends say,
Even the cattle kneel to pray,
Even the beasts of wood and field
Homage to Christ the Saviour yield.
Horse and cow and woolly sheep
Wake themselves from their heavy sleep,
Bending heads and knees to Him
Who came to earth in a stable dim.
Far away in the forest dark
Creatures timidly wake and hark,
Feathered bird and furry beast
Turn their eyes to the mystic East.
Loud at the dawning, chanticleer
Sounds his note, the rest of the year,
But Christmas Eve the whole night long
Honouring Christ he sings his song.
Christmas morn, the legends say,
Even the cattle kneel to pray,
Even the wildest beast afar
Knows the light of the Saviour's star.

But Give Me Holly
Christina Rossetti

But give me holly, bold and jolly,
Honest, prickly, shining holly;
Pluck me holly leaf and berry
For the day when I make merry.

BEFORE DAWN
Walter de la Mare

Dim-berried is the mistletoe
With globes of sheenless grey,
The holly mid ten thousand thorns
Smoulders its fires away;
And in the manger Jesu sleeps
This Christmas Day.

Bull unto bull with hollow throat
Makes echo every hill,
Cold sheep in pastures thick with snow
The air with bleatings fill;
While of his mother's heart this Babe
Takes His sweet will.

All flowers and butterflies lie hid,
The blackbird and the thrush
Pipe but as a little as they flit

Restless from bush to bush;
Even to the robin Gabriel hath
Cried softly, 'Hush!'

Now night is astir with burning stars
In darkness of the snow;
Burdened with frankincense and myrrh
And gold the strangers go
Into a dusk where one dim lamp
Burns faintly, Lo!

No snowdrop yet its small head nods,
In winds of winter drear;
No lark at casement in the sky
Sings matins shrill and clear;
Yet in this frozen mirk the Dawn
Breathes, Spring is here!

CHRISTMAS GREETING
Author Unknown

Sing hey! Sing hey!
For Christmas Day;
Twine mistletoe and holly,
For friendship glows
In winter snows,
And so let's all be jolly.

BE MERRY ALL
W. R. Spencer

Be merry all,
Be merry all,
With holly dress the festive hall;
Prepare the song,
The feast, the ball,
To welcome merry Christmas.

A MERRY CHRISTMAS

CHAPTER FIVE

THE PROMISE TO MARY

LUKE 1:26-35, 38

And in the sixth month the angel Gabriel was sent from God unto a city of Galilee, named Nazareth, To a virgin espoused to a man whose name was Joseph, of the house of David; and the virgin's name was Mary. And the angel came in unto her, and said, Hail, thou that art highly favoured, the Lord is with thee: blessed art thou among women. And when she saw him, she was troubled at his saying, and cast in her mind what manner of salutation this should be. And the angel said unto her, Fear not, Mary: for thou hast found favour with God. And, behold, thou shalt conceive in thy womb, and bring forth a son, and shalt call his name JESUS. He shall be great, and shall be called the Son of the Highest: and the Lord God shall give unto him the throne of his father David: And he shall reign over the house of Jacob for ever; and of his kingdom there shall be no end. Then said Mary unto the angel, How shall this be, seeing I know not a man? And the angel answered and said unto her, The Holy Ghost shall come upon thee, and the power of the Highest shall overshadow thee: therefore also that holy thing which shall be born of thee shall be called the Son of God. And Mary said, Behold the handmaid of the Lord; be it unto me according to thy word. And the angel departed from her.

Angels from The Realms of Glory

James Montgomery

Henry Thomas Smart

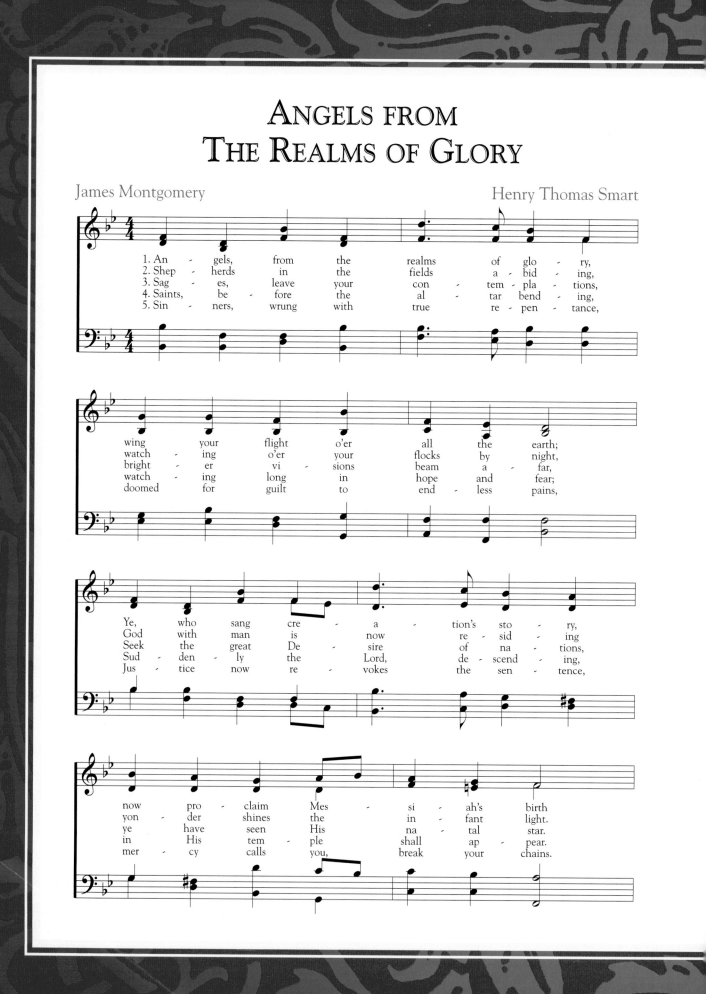

Christmas is here;
Winds whistle shrill,
Icy and chill:
Little care we
Little we fear
Weather without,
Sheltered about
The Mahogany tree.

W.M. THACKERAY.

Evenings we knew,
Happy as this;
Faces we miss,
Pleasant to see.
Kind hearts and true,
Gentle and just,
Peace to your dust!
We sing round the tree.

MARCUS WARD & CO.

Come and wor - ship! Come and wor - ship!
Wor - ship Christ the new - born King!

MARY'S SON
George MacDonald

They all were looking for a king
To slay their foes and lift them high:
Thou cam'st, a little baby thing
That made a woman cry.

MARY'S SONG
Charles Causley

Sleep, King Jesus;
Your royal bed
Is made of hay
In a cattle-shed.
Sleep, King Jesus;
Do not fear,
Joseph is watching
And waiting near.

Warm in the wintry air
You lie,
The ox and the donkey
Standing by.

With summer eyes
They seem to say:
Welcome, Jesus,
On Christmas Day!

Sleep, King Jesus;
Your diamond crown
High in the sky
Where the stars look down.
Let your reign
Of love begin,
That all the world
May enter in.

A Holy Happy Christmastide.

Annunciation
John Donne

Salvation to all that will is nigh;
That All, which always is All everywhere,
Which cannot sin, and yet all sins must bear,
Which cannot die, yet cannot choose but die,
Lo, faithful Virgin, yields himself to lie
In prison, in thy womb; and though he there
Can take no sin, nor thou give, yet he'll wear,
Taken from thence, flesh, which death's force may try.
Ere by the spheres time was created, thou
Wast in his mind, who is thy Son, and Brother;
Whom thou conceiv'st, conceiv'd; yea thou art now
Thy Maker's maker, and thy Father's mother;
Thou hast light in dark; and shut in little room,
Immensity cloistered in thy dear womb.

Christmas Prayer
Joyce Huggett

Lord Jesus, this Christmas as we sing the familiar carols, hear the familiar reading, and ponder on familiar mysteries, give to us the gift of pure worship—that ability which Mary had of attributing to you your true worth, your full value, your inestimable greatness.

Teach us to be reverent; yet teach us how to express the love that burns within our hearts as we think of your goodness to us—that you have come to be our light in darkness, our hope in despair, our strength in weakness, our shelter in the storm—yes, and our eternal Saviour.

Country Carols

Laurie Lee

We approached our last house high up on the hill, the place of Joseph the farmer. For him we had chosen a special carol, which was about the other Joseph, so that we always felt that singing it added a spicy cheek to the night. The last stretch of country to reach his farm was perhaps the most difficult of all. In these rough, bare lanes, open to all winds, sheep were buried and wagons lost. Huddled together, we tramped in one another's footsteps, powdered snow blew into our screwed-up eyes, the candles burned low, some blew out altogether, and we talked loudly above the gale.

Crossing, at last, the frozen mill-stream—whose wheel in summer still turned a barren mechanism—we climbed up to Joseph's farm. Sheltered by trees, warm on its bed of snow, it seemed always to be like this. As always it was late; as always this was our final call. The snow had a fine crust upon it, and the old trees sparkled like tinsel. We grouped ourselves round the farmhouse porch. The sky cleared, and broad streams of stars ran down over the valley and away to Wales. On Slad's white slope, seen through the black sticks of its woods, some red lamps still burned in the windows.

Everything was quiet; everywhere there was the faint, crackling silence of the winter night. We started singing, and we were all moved by the words and the sudden trueness of our voices. Pure, very clear, and breathless we sang:

> As Joseph was a-walking
> He heard an angel sing,
> 'This night shall be the birth-time
> Of Christ the Heavenly King.
>
> 'He neither shall be borned
> In Housen nor in hall,
> Nor in a place of paradise
> But in an ox's stall. . . .'

And two thousand Christmases became real to us then; the houses, the halls, the places of paradise had all been visited; the stars were bright to guide the Kings through the snow; and across the farmyard we could hear the beasts in their stalls. We were given roast apples and hot mince pies, in our nostrils were the spices like myrrh, and in our wooden box, as we headed back for the village, there were golden gifts for all.

What Child Is This?

William Chatterton Dix

Greensleeves

CHRISTMAS HYMN
Eugene Field

Sing, Christmas bells!
Say to the earth this is the morn
Whereon our Saviour-King is born;
Sing to all men—the bond, the free,
The rich, the poor, the high, the low,
The little child that sports in glee,
The aged folk that tottering go—
Proclaim the morn
That Christ is born,
That saveth them and saveth me!

Sing, sons of earth!
O ransomed seed of Adam, sing!
God liveth, and we have a king!
The curse is gone, the bound are free—
By Bethlehem's star that brightly beamed,
By all the heavenly signs that be,
We know that Israel is redeemed;
That on this morn
The Christ is born
That saveth you and saveth me!

Sing, O my heart!
Sing thou in rapture this dear morn
Whereon the blessed Prince is born!
And as thy songs shall be of love,
So let my deeds be charity—
By the dear Lord that reigns above,
By Him that died upon the tree,
By this fair morn
Whereon is born
The Christ that saveth all and me!

At Thy Nativity
John Milton

At thy Nativity a glorious choir
Of Angels in the field of Bethlehem sung
To Shepherds watching at their folds by night,
And told them the Messiah now was born,
Where they might see him, and to thee they came;
Directed to the Manger where thou lais't,
For in the Inn was left no better room:
A Star, not seen before in Heaven appearing
Guided the Wise Men thither from the East,
To honour thee with Incense, Myrrh, and Gold,
By whose bright course led on they found the place,
Affirming it thy Star new grav'n in Heaven,
By which they knew thee King of Israel born.

The Heart of Mary
Sheldon Vanauken

Dear sister, I was human not divine,
The angel left me woman as before,
And when, like flame beneath my heart, I bore
The Son, I was the vestal and the shrine.
My arms held Heaven at my breast—not wine
But milk made blood, in which no mothering doubt
Prefigured patterns of the pouring out,
O Lamb! to stain the world incarnadine.
The Magi saw a crown that lay ahead,
But not the bitter glory of the reign;
They called him King and knelt among the kine.
I pondered in my heart what they had said,
Yet could not see the bloody cup of pain.
I was but woman—though my God was mine.

CHAPTER SIX

THE SAVIOUR IS BORN

LUKE 2:1, 3-7

And it came to pass in those days, that there went out a decree from Caesar Augustus that all the world should be taxed. And all went to be taxed, every one into his own city. And Joseph also went up from Galilee, out of the city of Nazareth, into Judaea, unto the city of David, which is called Bethlehem (because he was of the house and lineage of David); To be taxed with Mary his espoused wife, being great with child. And so it was, that, while they were there, the days were accomplished that she should be delivered. And she brought forth her firstborn son, and wrapped him in swaddling clothes, and laid him in a manger; because there was no room for them in the inn.

Away in a Manger

1-2, Little Children's Book for Schools and Family;3, Charles H. Gabriel   James R. Murray

lay,　　　The　lit - tle Lord　Je - sus　a -
sky,　　　And　stay　by my　cra - dle till
care,　　　And　take　us to　heav - en,　to

sleep　　on　　the　　hay.
morn - ing　with　is　　nigh.
live　　with　Thee　there.

FROM HEAVEN HIGH

Martin Luther
Translated by Roland H. Bainton

From heaven high I come to earth;
I bring good tidings of great mirth:
This mirth is such a wondrous thing
That I must tell you all and sing.

A little child for you this morn
Has from a chosen maid been born;
A little child so tender, sweet,
That you should skip upon your feet.

How glad we'll be that this is so!
With all the shepherds, let us go
To see what God for us has done
In sending us his own dear Son.

Look, look, my heart, and let me peek:
Whom in the manger do you seek?
Who is that lovely little one?
The baby Jesus, God's own Son.

Be welcome, Lord! Be now our guest:
By you poor sinners have been blessed,
In nakedness and cold you lie:
How can I thank you; how can I?

You wanted so to make me know
That you had let all great things go;
You had a palace in the sky:
You left it there for such as I.

And if the world were twice as wide,
With gold and precious jewels inside,
Still such a cradle would not do
To hold a babe so great as you.

A Merry CHRISTMAS

CHRIST IS BORN
Margaret Deland

At the break of Christmas Day,
Through the frosty starlight ringing,
Faint and sweet and far away,
Comes the sound of children, singing,
Chanting, singing,
"Cease to mourn,
For Christ is born,
Peace and joy to all men bringing!"

Careless that the chill winds blow,
Growing stronger, sweeter, clearer,
Noiseless footfalls in the snow
Bring the happy voices nearer;
Hear them singing,
"Winter's drear,
But Christ is here,
Mirth and gladness with Him bringing!"

"Merry Christmas!" hear them say,
As the East is growing lighter;
"May the joy of Christmas Day
Make your whole year gladder, brighter!"
Join their singing,
"To each home
Our Christ has come,
All Love's treasures with Him bringing!"

A Christmas Hymn

Author Unknown

In the fields where, long ago,
Dropping tears amid the leaves,
Ruth's young feet went to and fro,
Binding up the scattered sheaves,
In the field that heard the voice
Of Judea's shepherd King,
Still the gleaners may rejoice,
Still the reapers shout and sing.

For each mount and vale and plain
Felt the touch of holier feet.
Then the gleaners of the grain
Heard, in voices full and sweet,
"Peace on earth, good will to men,"
Ring from angel lips afar,
While, o'er every glade and glen,
Broke the light of Bethlehem's star.

Star of hope to souls in night,
Star of peace above our strife,
Guiding, where the gates of death
Ope to fields of endless life.
Wanderer from the nightly throng
Which the eastern heavens gem;
Guided, by an angel's song,
To the Babe of Bethlehem.

Not Judea's hills alone
Have earth's weary gleaners trod,
Not to heirs of David's throne
Is it given to "reign with God."
But where'er on His green earth
Heavenly faith and longing are,
Heavenly hope and life have birth,
'Neath the smile of Bethlehem's star.

In each lowly heart or home,
By each love-watched cradle-bed,
Where we rest, or where we roam,
Still its changeless light is shed.
In its beams each quickened heart,
Howe'er saddened or denied,
Keeps one little space apart
For the Hebrew mother's Child.

And that inner temple fair
May be holier ground than this,
Hallowed by the pilgrim's prayer,
Warmed by many a pilgrim's kiss.
In its shadow still and dim,
Where our holiest longings are,
Rings forever Bethlehem's hymn,
Shines forever Bethlehem's star.

O Holy Night

Placide Clappeau; Trans. John S. Dwight

Adolphe Charles Adam

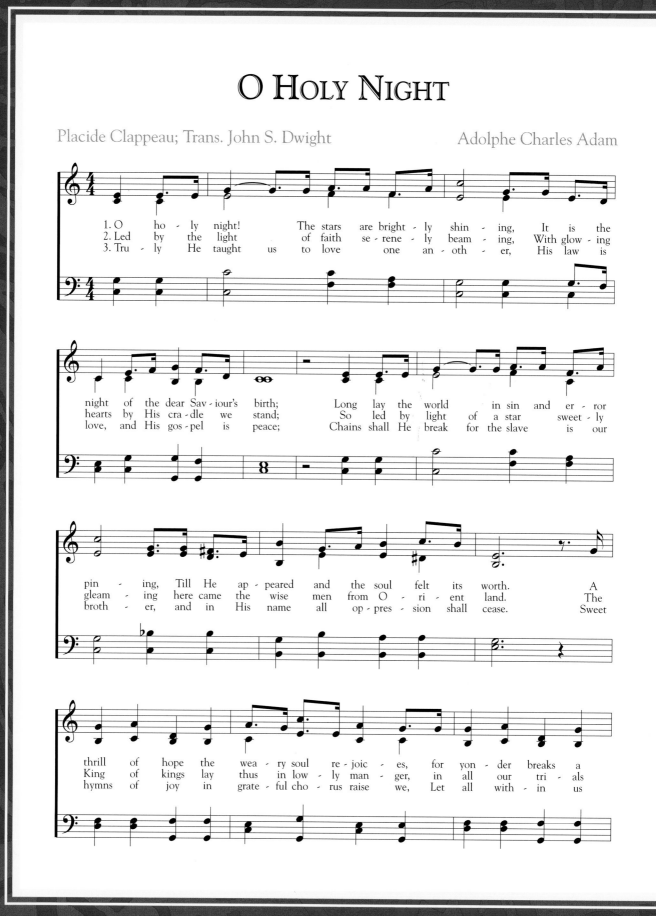

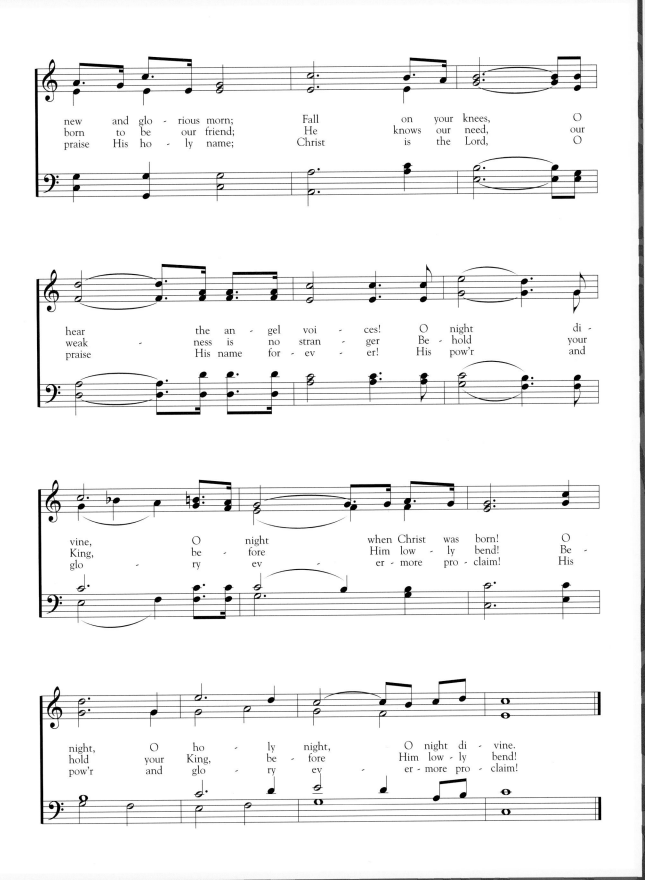

THE HOUSE OF CHRISTMAS
G. K. Chesterton

There fared a mother driven forth
Out of an inn to roam;
In the place where she was homeless
All men are at home.
The crazy stable close at hand,
With shaking timber and shifting sand,
Grew a stronger thing to abide and stand
Than the square stones of Rome.

For men are homesick in their homes,
And strangers under the sun,

And they lay their heads in a foreign land
Whenever the day is done.
Here we have battle and blazing eyes,
And chance and honour and high surprise,
But our homes are under miraculous skies
Where the yule tale was begun.

A child in a foul stable,
Where the beasts feed and foam;
Only where He was homeless
Are you and I at home;

We have hands that fashion and heads
    that know,
But our hearts we lost—how long ago!
In a place no chart nor ship can show
Under the sky's dome.

This world is wild as an old wife's tale,
And strange the plain things are,
The earth is enough and the air is enough
For our wonder and our war;
But our rest is as far as the fire-drake swings
And our peace is put in impossible things

Where clashed and thundered
    unthinkable wings
Round an incredible star.

To an open house in the evening
Home shall all men come,
To an older place than Eden
And a taller town than Rome.
To the end of the way of the wandering star,
To the things that cannot be and that are,
To the place where God was homeless
And all men are at home.

CHRISTMAS DAY

Washington Irving

When I woke the next morning . . . I heard the sound of little feet pattering outside of the door, and a whispering consultation. Presently a choir of small voices chanted forth an old Christmas carol, the burden of which was:

> Rejoice, our Savior he was born
>
> On Christmas day in the morning.

I rose softly, slipt on my clothes, opened the door suddenly, and beheld one of the most beautiful little fairy groups that a painter could imagine. It consisted of a boy and two girls, the eldest not more than six, and lovely as seraphs. They were going the rounds of the house, and singing at every chamber door; but my sudden appearance frightened them into mute bashfulness. They remained for a moment playing on their lips with their fingers, and now and then stealing a shy glance from under their eyebrows, until, as if by one impulse, they scampered away, and as they turned an angle of the gallery, I heard them laughing in triumph at their escape.

I had scarcely dressed myself, when a servant appeared to invite me to family prayers. He showed me the way to a small chapel in the old wing of the house, where I found the principal part of the family already assembled. . . . The service was followed by a Christmas carol, which Mr. Bracebridge himself had constructed from a poem of his favorite author, Herrick; and it had been adapted to an old church melody by Master Simon. As there were several good voices among the household, the effect was extremely pleasing; but I was particularly gratified by the exaltation of heart, and sudden sally of grateful feeling, with which the worthy squire delivered one stanza; his eye glistening, and his voice rambling out of all the bounds of time and tune:

> 'Tis thou that crown'st my glittering
>   hearth
> With guiltlesse mirth,
> And givest me Wassaile bowles to drink
> Spiced to the brink:
> Lord, 'tis thy plenty-dropping hand
> That soiles my land:
> And giv'st me for my bushell sowne,
> Twice ten for one.

I afterwards understood that early morning service was read on every Sunday and saints' day throughout the year, either by Mr. Bracebridge or by some member of the family. It was once almost universally the case at the seats of the nobility and gentry of England, and it is much to be regretted that the custom is falling into neglect; for the dullest observer must be sensible of the order and serenity prevalent in those households, where the occasional exercise of a beautiful form of worship in the morning gives, as it were, the keynote to every temper for the day, and attunes every spirit to harmony.

While we were talking we heard the distant tolling of the village bell, and I was told that the squire was a little particular in having his household at church on a Christmas morning; considering it a day of pouring out of thanks and rejoicing; for, as old Tusser observed,

> At Christmas be merry,
> and thankful withal,
> And feast thy poor
> neighbors, the great
> with the small.

As the morning, though frosty, was remarkably fine and clear, most of the family walked to the church, which was a very old building of gray stone, and stood near a village, about half a mile from the park gate. . . . The elder folks gathered in knots in the church-yard, greeting and shaking hands; and the children ran about crying Ule! Ule! and repeating some uncouth rhymes, which the parson, who had joined us, informed me had been handed down from days of yore. The villagers doffed their hats to the squire as he passed, giving him the good wishes of the season with every appearance of heart-felt sincerity, and were invited by him to the hall, to take

something to keep out the cold of the weather; and I heard blessings uttered by several of the poor, which convinced me that, in the midst of his enjoyments, the worthy old cavalier had not forgotten the true Christmas virtue of charity.

CHAPTER SEVEN

THE SHEPHERDS WORSHIP

LUKE 2:8-16

And there were in the same country shepherds abiding in the field, keeping watch over their flock by night. And, lo, the angel of the Lord came upon them, and the glory of the Lord shone round about them: and they were sore afraid. And the angel said unto them, Fear not: for, behold, I bring you good tidings of great joy, which shall be to all people. For unto you is born this day in the city of David a Saviour, which is Christ the Lord. And this shall be a sign unto you; Ye shall find the babe wrapped in swaddling clothes, lying in a manger. And suddenly there was with the angel a multitude of the heavenly host praising God, and saying, Glory to God in the highest, and on earth peace, good will toward men. And it came to pass, as the angels were gone away from them into heaven, the shepherds said one to another, Let us now go even unto Bethlehem, and see this thing which is come to pass, which the Lord hath made known unto us. And they came with haste, and found Mary, and Joseph, and the babe lying in a manger.

In the Bleak Midwinter

Christina Rossetti   Gustav Holst

Snow had fall - en, snow on snow,
In nough for Him, Whom an - gels
But His moth - er on - ly,
If I were a wise man,

snow on snow,
sta - ble - place suf - ficed
fall in her maid - en bliss,
I would do my part;
The
The
Yet

In the bleak mid - win - ter,
Lord God in - car - nate,
ox and ass and cam - el
what I can I give Him,

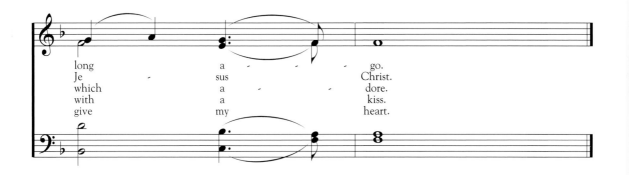

long a - go.
Je - sus Christ.
which a - dore.
with a kiss.
give my heart.

Noel: Christmas Eve, 1913
Robert Bridges

A frosty Christmas Eve when the stars were shining
Faced I forth alone where westward falls the hill,
And from many a village in the water'd valley
Distant music reach'd me, peals of bells aringing;
The constellated sound ran sprinkling on earth's floor
As the dark vault about with stars was spangled o'er.

Then sped my thought to keep that first Christmas of all
When the shepherds watching by their fold ere dawn
Heard music in the fields and marveling could not tell
Whether it were angels or the bright stars singing.

Now blessed be the tow'rs that crown England so fair
That stand up strong in prayer unto God for our souls:
Blessed be their founders (said I) an' our country folk
Who are ringing for Christ in the belfries to-night
With arms lifted to clutch the rattling ropes that race
Into the dark above and the mad, romping din.

But to me heard afar it was starry music,
Angels' song, comforting as the comfort of Christ
When he spake tenderly to his sorrowful flock:
The old words came to me by the riches of time
Mellow'd and transfigured as I stood on the hill
Heark'ning in the aspect of th' eternal silence.

O God the Son

Frank Colquhoun

O God the Son, highest and holiest, who didst humble thyself to share our birth and our death: Bring us with the shepherd and wise men to kneel before thy lowly cradle, that we may come to sing with thine angels thy glorious praises in heaven; where with the Father and the Holy Spirit thou livest and reignest God, world without end.

Carols in the Lamplight

Kenneth Grahame

At last the Rat succeeded in decoying Mole to the table, and had just got seriously to work with the sardine-opener when sounds were heard from the fore-court without— sounds like the scuffling of small feet in the gravel and a confused murmur of tiny voices, while broken sentences reached them— "Now, all in a line—Hold the lantern up a bit, Tommy—Clear your throats first—No coughing after I say one, two, three— Where's young Bill?—Here, come on, do, we're all a-waiting—"

"What's up?" inquired the Rat, pausing in his labours.

"I think it must be the field-mice," replied the Mole, with a touch of pride in his manner. "They go round carol-singing regularly at this time of the year. They're quite an institution in these parts. And they never pass me over—they come to Mole End last of all; and I used to give them hot drinks, and supper too sometimes, when I could afford it. It will be like old times to hear them again."

"Let's have a look at them!" cried the Rat, jumping up and running to the door.

It was a pretty sight, and a seasonable one, that met their eyes when they flung the door open. In the fore-court, lit by the dim rays of a horn lantern, some eight or ten little field-mice stood in a semicircle, red worsted comforters round their throats, their fore-paws thrust deep into their pockets, their feet jigging for warmth. With bright, beady eyes they glanced shyly at each other, sniggering a little, sniffing and applying coat sleeves a good deal. As the door opened, one of the elder ones that carried the lantern was just saying, "Now then, one, two, three!" and forthwith their shrill little voices uprose on the air, singing one of the old-time carols that their forefathers composed in fields that were fallow and held by frost, or when snow-bound in chimney corners, and handed down to be sung in the miry street to lamp-lit windows at Yule-time.

The voices ceased, the singers, bashful but smiling, exchanged sidelong glances, and silence succeeded—but for a moment only. Then, from up above and far away, down the tunnel they had so lately travelled was borne to their ears in a faint, musical hum the sound of distant bells ringing a joyful and clangorous peal.

"Very well sung, boys!" cried the Rat heartily. "And now come along in, all of you, and warm yourselves by the fire, and have something hot!"

THE MICE'S CAROL
Kenneth Grahame

Villagers all, this frosty tide,
Let your doors swing open wide,
Though wind may follow, and snow beside,
Yet draw us in by your fire to bide;
Joy shall be yours in the morning!

Here we stand in the cold and the sleet,
Blowing fingers and stamping feet,
Come from far away you to greet—
You by the fire and we in the street—
Bidding you joy in the morning!

For ere one half of the night was gone,
Sudden a star has led us on,
Raining bliss and benison—

Bliss to-morrow and more anon,
Joy for every morning!

Goodman Joseph toiled through the snow—
Saw the star o'er a stable low;
Mary she might not further go—
Welcome thatch, and litter below!
Joy was hers in the morning!

And then they heard the angels tell
'Who were the first to cry Noel?
Animals all, as it befell,
In the stable where they did dwell!
Joy shall be theirs in the morning!'

REMEMBERING CAROLS
Charles Lamb

Let us have leave to remember the festivities at Christmas, when the richest of us would club our stock to have a gaudy day, sitting round the fire, replenished to the height with logs; and the penniless, and he that could contribute nothing, partook in all the mirth, and in some of the substantialities of the feasting; the carol sung by night at that time of the year, which, when a young boy, I have so often lain awake to hear from seven (the hour of going to bed) till ten when it was sung by the older boys and monitors, and have listened to it, in their rude chanting, till I have been transported in fancy to the fields of Bethlehem, and the song which was sung at that season by angels' voices to the shepherds.

GOD REST YOU MERRY, GENTLEMEN

English Traditional

Arr. John Stainer

we were gone a - stray:
noth - ing take in   scorn
Son of God by name:
friends of Sa - tan quite:"
bless - ed Babe to find:
to the Lord did pray:
oth - ers doth de - face:

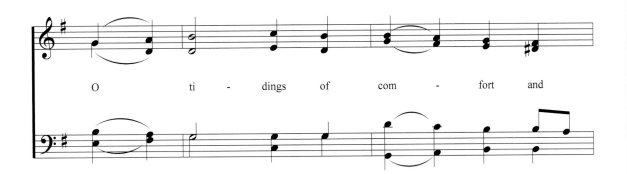

O ti - dings of com - fort and

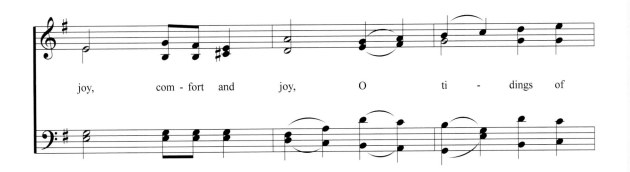

joy, com - fort and joy, O ti - dings of

com - fort and joy.

A Christmas Carol for Children

Martin Luther

Good news from heaven the angels bring,
Glad tiding to the earth they sing:
To us this day a child is given,
To crown us with the joy of heaven.

This is the Christ, our God and Lord,
Who in all need shall aid afford;
He will Himself our Saviour be,
From sin and sorrow set us free.

To us that blessedness He brings,
Which from the Father's bounty springs:
That in the heavenly realm we may
With Him enjoy eternal day.

All hail, Thou noble Guest, this morn,
Whose love did not the sinner scorn!

In my distress Thou cam'st to me:
What thanks shall I return to Thee?

Were earth a thousand time as fair,
Beset with gold and jewels rare,
She yet were far too poor to be
A narrow cradle, Lord, for Thee.

Ah, dearest Jesus, Holy Child!
Make Thee a bed soft, undefiled,
Within my heart, that it may be
A quiet chamber kept for Thee.

Praise God upon His heavenly throne,
Who gave to us His only Son:
For this His hosts on joyful wing,
A blest New Year of mercy sing.

Christmas Chant

Isabel Shaw

Candle, candle
Burning bright
On our window
Sill tonight,
Like the shining
Christmas star

Guiding shepherds
From afar,
Lead some weary
Traveler here,
That he may share
Our Christmas cheer.

FOR CHRISTMAS DAY
Eleanor Farjeon

A carol round the ruddy hearth,
A song outside the door—
Let Christmas Day make sure its lay
Sounds sweetly to the poor.

A turkey in the baking-tin,
A pudding in the pot—
Let Christmas Day the hunger stay
In them that have not got.

Red berries on the picture-frame,
White berries in the hall—
Let Christmas Day look twice as gay
With evergreens for all.

A stocking on the chimney piece,
A present on the chair—
Let Christmas Day not pass away
Till those who have do share.

A star upon the midnight sky,
A shepherd looking East—
On Christmas Day let all men pray,
And not till after feast.

CHAPTER EIGHT

A Star in The East

Matthew 2:1-12

Now when Jesus was born in Bethlehem of Judaea in the days of Herod the king, behold, there came wise men from the east to Jerusalem, Saying, Where is he that is born King of the Jews? for we have seen his star in the east, and are come to worship him. When Herod the king had heard these things, he was troubled, and all Jerusalem with him. And when he had gathered all the chief priests and scribes of the people together, he demanded of them where Christ should be born. And they said unto him, In Bethlehem of Judaea: for thus it is written by the prophet, And thou Bethlehem, in the land of Juda, art not the least among the princes of Juda: for out of thee shall come a Governor, that shall rule my people Israel. Then Herod, when he had privily called the wise men, enquired of them diligently what time the star appeared. And he sent them to Bethlehem, and said, Go and search diligently for the young child; and when ye have found him, bring me word again, that I may come and worship him also. When they had heard the king, they departed; and, lo, the star, which they saw in the east, went before them, till it came and stood over where the young child was. When they saw the star, they rejoiced with exceeding great joy. And when they were come into the house, they saw the young child with Mary his mother, and fell down, and worshiped him: and

when they had opened their treasures, they presented unto him gifts; gold, and
frankincense, and myrrh. And being warned of God in a dream that they should
not return to Herod, they departed into their own country another way.

THE FIRST NOEL

Traditional English

Arr. John Stainer

sheep,   on a cold win - ter's night   that was so deep:
light,   and so it con - tin - ued both day and night:
tent,   and to fol - low the star wher - ev - er it went:
stay,   right o - ver the place where Je - sus lay:
see,   and found the Babe in po - ver - ty:
ence,   their gold, and myrrh, and frank - in - cense:
lay   all in a man - ger, a - mong the hay:
nought,   and with His blood man - king hath bought.
all   a rest - ing place in gen - er - al:

No - el, No - el, No - el, No - el,

Born is the King of Is - ra - el.

Out of the Shadow of the Night
Michael Fairless

Out of the Shadow of the Night
I come, led by the starshine bright,
With broken heart to bring to Thee
The fruit of Thine epiphany.
The gift my fellows send by me,
The myrrh to bed Thine agony,
I set it here beneath Thy feet,
In token of Death's great defeat;
And hail Thee Conqueror in the strife,
And hail Thee Lord of light and life.
All hail! All hail the virgin Son!
All hail! Thou little helpless One!
All hail! Thou King upon the tree!
All hail! The Babe on Mary's knee,
The center of all mystery!

The Wise Men Ask the Children the Way
Heinrich Heine
Translated by Geoffrey Grigson

'Dear children,' they asked in every town,
Three kings from the land of the sun.
'Which is the road to Bethlehem?'
But neither the old nor the young
Could tell, and the kings rode on:
Their guide was a star in the air
Of gold, which glittered ahead of them.
So clear, so clear.
The star stood still over Joseph's house.
They all of them stepped in:
The good ox lowed and the little child cried,
And the kings began to sing.

CHRISTMAS, 1862

Alexander Smith

This, then, is Christmas, 1862. . . . Through the clear, wintry sunshine the bells this morning rang from the gray church tower amid the leafless elms, and up the walk the villagers trooped in their best dresses and their best faces—the latter a little reddened by the sharp wind: mere redness in the middle aged; in the maids, wonderful bloom to the eyes of their lovers—and took their places decently in the ancient pews.

The clerk read the beautiful prayers of our Church, which seem more beautiful at Christmas than at any other period. For that very feeling which breaks down at this time the barriers which custom, birth, or wealth have erected between man and man, strike down the barrier of time which intervenes between the worshiper of today and the great body of worshipers who are at rest in their graves. On such a day as this, hearing these prayers, we feel a kinship with the devout generations who heard them long ago.

Prayers over, the clergyman—who is no Boanerges, of Chrysostom, golden-mouthed, but a loving, genial-hearted, pious man, the whole extent of his life from his boyhood until now full of charity and kindly deeds, as autumn fields with heavy wheaten ears; the clergyman, I say—for the sentence is becoming unwieldy on my hands, and one must double back to secure connexion—read out in that silvery voice of his, which is sweeter than any music to my ear, those chapters of the New Testament that deal with the birth of the Saviour. And the red-faced rustic congregation hung on the good man's voice as he spoke of the Infant brought forth in a manger, of the shining angels that appeared in the mid-air to the shepherd, of the miraculous star that took its station in the sky, and of the wise men who came from afar and laid their gifts of frankincense and myrrh at the feet of the child.

With the story every one was familiar, but on that day, and backed by the persuasive melody of the reader's voice, it seemed to all quite new—at least, they listened attentively as if it were. The discourse that followed possessed no remarkable thoughts; it dealt simply with the goodness of the Maker of heaven and earth, and the shortness of time, with the duties of thankfulness and charity to the poor; and I am persuaded that every one who heard returned to his house in a better frame of mind.

WE THREE KINGS

John Henry Hopkins, Jr.   John Henry Hopkins, Jr.

1. We three kings of O - ri - ent are,
2. Born a King on Beth - le - hem's plain,
3. Frank - in - cense to of - fer have I,
4. Myrrh is mine, its bit - ter per - fume
5. Glo - rious now be - hold Him a - rise,

bear - ing gifts we trav - erse a - far,
gold I bring, to crown Him a - gain,
in - cense owns a De - i - ty nigh.
breathes a life of gath - er - ing gloom;
King and God and Sac - ri - fice,

Field and foun - tain, moor and moun - tain,
King for ev - er ceas - ing nev - er
Pray'r and prais - ing all men rais - ing,
Sor - r'wing, sigh - ing, bleed - ing, dy - ing,
Al - le - lu - ia, Al - le - lu - ia,

fol - low - ing yon - der star.
o - ver us all to reign.
wor - ship Him, God most high.
sealed in the stone - cold tomb.
earth to the heav'ns re - plies.

THE GLAD EVANGEL

Kate Douglas Wiggin

When the Child of Nazareth was born, the sun, according to the Bosnian legend, "leaped in the heavens, and the stars around it danced. A peace came over mountain and forest. Even the rotten stump stood straight and healthy on the green hill-side. The grass was beflowered with open blossoms, incense sweet as myrrh pervaded upland and forest, birds sang on the mountain top, and all gave thanks to the great God."

It is naught but an old folk-tale, but it has truth hidden at its heart, for a strange, subtle force, a spirit of genial good will, a new-born kindness, seems to animate child and man alike when the world pays its tribute to the "heaven-sent youngling," as the poet Drummond calls the infant Christ.

When the three Wise Men rode from the East into the West on that "first, best Christmas night," they bore on their saddle-bows three caskets filled with gold and frankincense and myrrh, to be laid at the feet of the manger-cradled babe of Bethlehem. Beginning with this old, old journey, the spirit of giving crept into the world's heart. As the Magi came bearing gifts, so do we also; gifts that relieve want, gifts that are sweet and fragrant with friendship, gifts that breathe love, gifts that mean service, gifts inspired still by the star that shone over the City of David nearly two thousand years ago.

Then hang the green coronet of the Christmas-tree with glittering baubles and jewels of flame; heap offering on its emerald branches; bring the Yule log to the firing; deck the house with holly and mistletoe,

"And all the bells on earth shall ring
On Christmas day in the morning."

A BRIGH

AND JOYOUS CHRISTMAS.

THE THREE KINGS
Henry Wadsworth Longfellow

Three Kings came riding from far away,
Melchior and Gaspar and Baltasar;
Three Wise Men out of the East were they,
And they travelled by night and they slept by day,
For their guide was a beautiful, wonderful star.

The star was so beautiful, large, and clear,
That all the other stars of the sky
Became a white mist in the atmosphere,
And by this they knew that the coming was near
Of the Prince foretold in the prophecy.

And so the Three Kings rode into the West,
Through the dusk of the night, over hill and dell,
And sometimes they nodded with beard on breast,
And sometimes talked, as they paused to rest,
With the people they met at some wayside well.

So they rode away; and the star stood still,
The only one in the grey of morn;
Yes, it stopped—it stood still of its own free will,
Right over Bethlehem on the hill,
The city of David, where Christ was born.

And the Three Kings rode through the gate and the guard,
Through the silent street, till their horses turned
And neighed as they entered the great inn-yard;
But the windows were closed, and the doors were barred,
And only a light in the stable burned.

And cradled there in the scented hay,
In the air made sweet by the breath of kine,
The little child in the manger lay,
The child that would be king one day
Of a kingdom not human, but divine.

CHAPTER NINE

BEHOLD
HIS GLORY

JOHN 1:1-14

In the beginning was the Word, and the Word was with God, and the Word was God. The same was in the beginning with God. All things were made by him; and without him was not any thing made that was made. In him was life; and the life was the light of men. And the light shineth in darkness; and the darkness comprehended it not. There was a man sent from God, whose name was John. The same came for a witness, to bear witness of the Light, that all men through him might believe. He was not that Light, but was sent to bear witness of that Light. That was the true Light, which lighteth every man that cometh into the world. He was in the world, and the world was made by him, and the world knew him not. He came unto his own, and his own received him not. But as many as received him, to them gave he power to become the sons of God, even to them that believe on his name: Which were born, not of blood, nor of the will of the flesh, nor of the will of man, but of God. And the Word was made flesh, and dwelt among us, (and we beheld his glory, the glory as of the only begotten of the Father,) full of grace and truth.

O Come, All Ye Faithful

Trans. Frederick Oakeley

John Francis Wade

A Christmas Carol
James Russell Lowell

"What means this glory round our feet,"
The Magi mused, "more bright than morn?"
And voices chanted, clear and sweet,
"Today the Prince of Peace is born!"

"What means that star," the Shepherds said,
"That brightens through the rocky glen?"
And angels, answering overhead,
Sang "Peace on earth, good will to men!"

'Tis eighteen hundred years and more
Since those sweet oracles were dumb;
We wait for him, like them of yore,
Alas! he seems so slow to come!

But it was said, in words of old,
No time or sorrow e'er shall dim,
That little children might be bold—
In perfect trust to come to him.

All round our feet shall shine
A light like that the Wise Men saw,
If we our loving wills incline
To that sweet Life which is the Law.

So shall we learn to understand
The simple faith of shepherds then,
And, clasping kindly hand in hand,
Sing "Peace on earth, good will to men!"

But they who do their souls no wrong,
But keep at eve the faith of morn,
Shall daily hear the angel song,
"Today the Prince of Peace is born!"

MUSIC ON CHRISTMAS MORNING

Anne Brontë

Music I love—but never strain
Could kindle raptures so divine,
So grief assuage, so conquer pain,
And rouse this pensive heart of mine
As that we hear on Christmas morn,
Upon the wintry breezes borne.

Though darkness still her empire keep,
And hours must pass, ere morning break;
From troubled dreams, or slumbers deep,
That music kindly bids us wake:
It calls us, with an angel's voice,
To wake, and worship, and rejoice;

To greet with joy the glorious morn,
Which angels welcomed long ago,
When our redeeming Lord was born,
To bring the light of heaven below;
The powers of darkness to dispel,
And rescue earth from death and hell.

While listening to that sacred strain,
My raptured spirit soars on high;
I seem to hear those songs again

Resounding through the open sky,
That kindled such divine delight,
In those who watched their flocks by night.

With them I celebrate His birth—
Glory to God, in highest heaven,
Good-will to men, and peace on earth,
To us a Saviour-king is given;
Our God is come to claim His own,
And Satan's power is overthrown!

A sinless God, for sinful men,
Descends to suffer and to bleed;
Hell must renounce its empire then;
The price is paid, the world is freed,
And Satan's self must now confess
That Christ has earned a right to bless:

Now holy peace may smile from heaven,
And heavenly truth from earth shall spring:
The captive's galling bonds are riven,
For our redeemer is our king;
And He that gave his blood for men
Will lead us home to God again.

The Word Made Flesh

Augustine of Hippo

For the Word was made flesh that Your Wisdom, by which You created all things, might give suck to our souls' infancy. For Your Word, the eternal Truth, towering above the highest parts of your creation, lifts up to Himself those that were cast down. He built for Himself here below a lowly house of our clay, that by it He might bring down from themselves and bring up to Himself those who were to be made subject, healing the swollenness of their pride and fostering their love; so that their self-confidence might grow no further but rather diminish, seeing the deity at their feet, humbled by the assumption of our coat of human nature: to the end that weary at last they might cast themselves down upon His humanity and rise again in its rising.

The True Christmas

Henry Vaughn

The brightness of this day we owe
Not unto music, masque, nor show,
Nor gallant furniture, nor plate;
But to the manger's mean estate.
His life while here, as well as birth,
Was but a check to pomp and mirth;
And all man's greatness you may see
Condemned by His humility.
Then leave your open house and noise,
To welcome Him with holy joys,
And the poor shepherd's watchfulness
Whom light and hymns from heaven did bless.
What you abound with, cast abroad
To those that want, and ease your load.
Who empties thus, will bring more in;
But riot is both loss and sin.
Dress finely what comes not in sight,
And then you keep your Christmas right.

Christmas.

"They saw the young child with Mary His mother, and fell down and worshipped Him." Matthew II - XI.

Hark! The Herald Angels Sing

Charles Wesley

Felix Mendelssohn-Bartholdy

Hark! the her - ald an - gels sing, "Glo - ry to the new - born King!"

THIS NIGHT OF NIGHTS

Leslie D. Weatherhead

On Christmas night, this night of nights, when thousands of us are reunited with our families, giving ourselves up to mirth and song, let us pause to pay honour to Him from whom all this happiness comes. Let us remember that this is Christmas, the festival of Christ. Let us, on the wings of those lovely carols, go back in imagination to that mystic, starlit night, when God spoke to the world a new word, the word that became flesh and dwelt among us, until, in a human life—full of love, full of tenderness, full of utter self-giving—the nature of God was fully revealed. . . .

I know how the churches have fallen into disfavour with some folk; but have we ever realized that, if we could remove from the fabric we call civilization all the influences which come from Christ, we should reduce it to a tattered and dirty rag? Perhaps only those of us who have lived in obscure places of the earth, such as an eastern village entirely untouched by the spirit of Christ, can realize just how awful life can be without His influence or how dark is that night which is unreached by the faintest glimmer of His grace. Do not let us forget on Christmas Day what we owe to Him!

It is His spirit which makes this day so wonderful. It is not merely the holiday spirit, for August does not produce anything like the spirit of goodwill which permeates Christmas Day. On that day, throughout the whole of Christendom, there is a new spirit in the air. And it comes from Him. . . .

Isn't it a thrilling thought? I like to think that dignified directors of important companies at this moment are wearing pink tissue-paper hats taken out of crackers. . . . Solemn doctors put aside their bedside manner and are tonight found on all fours on the carpet making farmyard noises which make the kiddies squeal with delight. . . . And, in spite of much unhappiness and want, war and its many hardships, and the loneliness of some to whom our hearts go out in greeting, wherever they are, it is true to say that life is happier, hearts are lighter, minds are quickened to deeds of love and thoughts of others. It is Christmas! . . .

Why can't this spirit be kept up? I don't mean the hilarity. I don't mean mince pies and crackers. There must be an end to them. But why must we let go of the spirit of unconquerable goodwill which holds our hearts at this hour? We need not. Listen to this bit of the good news: 'As many as received Him, to them gave He the right to become children of God.'

CAROL FOR THE LAST CHRISTMAS EVE
Norman Nicholson

The first night, the first night,
The night that Christ was born,
His mother looked in his eyes and saw
Her maker in her son.

The twelfth night, the twelfth night,
After Christ was born,
The Wise Men found the child and knew
Their search had just begun.

Eleven thousand, two fifty nights,
After Christ was born,
A dead man hung in the child's light
And the sun went down at noon.

Six hundred thousand or thereabout nights,
After Christ was born,
I look at you and you look at me
But the sky is too dark for us to see
And the world waits for the sun.

But the last night, the last night,
Since ever Christ was born,
What his mother knew will be known again,
And what was found by the Three Wise Men,
And the sun will rise and so may we,
On the last morn, on Christmas Morn,
Umpteen hundred and eternity.

INDEX